FOR THE
A TA

| | |
|---|---|
| **Far From You** | 6 |
| **Shambolic** | 8 |
| **Mr. Disorey** | 10 |
| **Natural Disaster** | 11 |
| **Dead To Me** | 12 |
| **Leave Me Alone, Please** | 13 |
| **Light Seekers** | 14 |
| **Mistake Or Design** | 15 |
| **As It Is** | 16 |
| **The Ineffable Web** | 17 |
| **Sins** | 18 |
| **A Distant Memory** | 19 |
| **Please Don't Bury Me** | 21 |
| **What Is This Life?** | 22 |
| **Made To Be Loved** | 23 |
| **Callous** | 24 |
| **Unraveling** | 25 |
| **Unworthy** | 26 |

| | |
|---|---|
| **Questions Of Peril** | **27** |
| **Am I There Yet?** | **28** |
| **Mock Me Not** | **30** |
| **Not Doing So Well** | **31** |
| **Hiraeth** | **32** |
| **Blind Leading The Blind** | **33** |
| **Dead Weight** | **34** |
| **Filthy Fridays** | **35** |
| **The Void Of Desolation** | **36** |
| **The Horror** | **37** |
| **A kind Of Man** | **38** |
| **When Love Is Young** | **39** |
| **The Dynasty** | **40** |
| **Painless** | **41** |
| **Legacies** | **43** |
| **I Denounce You** | **44** |
| **Nightly Prayer** | **45** |
| **Just You And I** | **46** |
| **Sights** | **47** |
| **Grace** | **48** |
| **Much Dismayed** | **50** |

| | |
|---|---|
| **Disappearing Act** | **51** |
| **An Excuse For A Life** | **52** |
| **Square One** | **53** |
| **The Concept of Liberty** | **54** |
| **Focus** | **55** |
| **X** | **56** |
| **Only You** | **57** |
| **Elijah** | **59** |
| **Searching For Love** | **60** |
| **I'll Never Let Go** | **61** |
| **All Paths Lead Back To You** | **62** |
| **Eons and Eons** | **63** |
| **Island garden paradise** | **64** |
| **Our Blessing** | **65** |
| **The Conqueror And The Conquered** | **66** |
| **All For You** | **67** |
| **Proof** | **68** |
| **On Those Indigo Nights** | **69** |
| **Sublime** | **70** |
| **Abhorrent Behavior** | **71** |
| **Always You** | **72** |

| | |
|---|---:|
| **Devotion Island** | 73 |
| **Answers** | 74 |
| **Sunshine** | 75 |
| **The Beach** | 76 |
| **Summer Daze** | 78 |
| **Close To You** | 79 |

# HELL

## Far From You

Don't extol my deeds they're far from right,
Under the stars I found the light and the words to lead the way,
It feels my heart's eroding, for my soul's in the mode of foreboding,
Seeking and searching for what I thought I knew,
Much further is the way,
I awake to a daunting day
And the only thing I see to be true is the fact I feel so far from you,
The train to hell shudders further,
In the heart of degradation,
Feeling remiss over all of this as it pulls in at every station,
I say I feel fine when I'm feeling sublime
And the same when my world collapses,
I search the sky and get lost in blue crying because I feel *far* from you.
How joyful those I love create,
I'm happy in this current state,
Smiles and affection warm the blood inside,
The world around us melts away and I wish it would last another day
Yet, the end is always due,
I wouldn't feel so awful If I weren't so far from you,
I strain in the face of envy and the ploys my brethren distill,
Gathering deep inside to muster some strength of will,
I can't bear to forsake my morals for the sake of those I love,
It feels as though I'm sacrificing the one who comes above,
And I strive to act on as chivalrous,
But my friends are completely oblivious,

And it pains me when I see they've no clue,
But what will always hurt more than anything is how far I feel from you.

## Shambolic

I thought I put my enemies in jail but they're in my mind like tripped out rogues
Gone off the rail,
So when I was at my mums I'd walk to my dealers and home so I could cry alone
On a road that's filled with mechanic manic stars polluting my eyes like steel bars
That clamp my feet and hands,
This pain it only expands with every timid fiery step,
I search the windows like a stranger looking in for that face on every bus
Searching every eye that looks back as we discuss our mutual ignorance of each other,
I move onto the other, unknown brother but look away from these beings
For I'm seeking another,
It grows in me like a ravaged tree
When not long ago it was merely a seed,
I feel sick but I'm only eating so I can smoke more weed
And succeed in numbing every tribulation,
That's sown and grown into this complication
That never reaches a desperate verdict,
I don't need to wipe my tears they're marring my view,
They're already see through
These stains on my face,
I accept with equanimity this desolate ability
To maintain my anonymity
From all that I love,

I've fought for tranquility
But I haven't the capability
To cull my hostility
So I walk on alone.

## Mr. Disorey

Mr. Disorey, you looked into an 8 ball once and told me all the answers
I'd ever asked for but worse than taking away the sweet bitter of my life
It hit me friend to the very core my anxe to rife and sour my mind,
They weren't even the right answers and now it seems you've made me blind,
How unkind all our problems are, aren't we the most wretchedly blessed?
Freed of our tests but still we're the misfortunistics never at rest
Of our incarcerated, complicated, decimated world,
I don't deserve to live my days in the nasty ways all unfurled
But yet I do, here is I, amongst my peers drunk and high,
On all the treasures we swapped for fools gold drizzled in poison of the worst to be sold
Chasing our tails instead of our souls, lacking up fumes
In a giddy laughter that we're bold enough to complain about after,
But don't we the right to complain when life's this easy?
The best of are men are nothing short of sleazy
And the women breeze along walking by breezily,
Don't test their morals it's mad what they replied,
The hypocrisy ironically is intolerably denied
And I deny it too, I tell you I deny it I do,
The easy peasy freebies were nothing but a curse on me and you,
Don't get me wrong I put my hands up to all and nothing
I've respect for the pain from the pained
But I care too for my own life's blissful, selfish, suffering.

## Natural Disaster

How I relish those tiny moments between things to do,
Where I can let my mind loose and linger on the abstruse
That somehow now thrill my days from the daily abuse,
I thought I bought what I ought to sought,
But I spent my money unwisely,
And I fought what I caught 'til money's down to naught
And I'm repeating the same day ill advisedly,
Past stormy upheavals and shining traumas
Where I suffer the ill fate from lack of restorers,
Due to the constant betrayal through that of the informers,
I'm a tired tormentee, from the disastrous natural disasters committee,
Dripping in discrepancy, a high level of dysfunctional empathy,
There's no one here to agree,
But the woebegone silence from my trusted devotee,
In a distant wind past the thick of glass,
On an empty border that divides the working class
I hear a sullen sound, coming from a broken ground
I'm swallowed up by trivial thought,
I thought I bought what I ought to sought
But I spent my money unwisely.

## Dead To Me

Oh darling I had so much hope for how things with us would be,
Yet after such little time you're already dead to me,
I was once your treasure
You'd fare any weather to be by my side in the dark,
So I gave into you,
I thought you were truth
But you stomped all over my heart,
So I take to my bed
Acting fine
Smiling sweetly
But dying inside
And still you didn't see,
This is why you're dead to me,
What were those dreams you planted in mind?
That were quickly forgotten in very short time,
I once remembered but now they're lost on the breeze,
Pointless memories of what used to be
Before you were dead to me,
I'm not saying I'm worth much but I'm worth more than this,
Did I stare into hell thinking it bliss?
I wanted your love but I wasn't worth the fight,
I guess it wasn't meant to be,
I'm clearly dead to you and you're definitely dead to me,
The love we shared was a real thing,
You threw us away like it was just a fling,
So you may as well be dead
Because I'm dead to you,
And the person who loved me, he's dead too.

## Leave Me Alone, Please

People keep letting the light in and opening my curtains for me,
They don't seem to understand I don't want to see,
I just want people to leave me be,
I turn my phone off and still it pings,
Do you know how annoying it is when it rings?
Do you know how annoying I find these things?
The problems of kings! I know,
They present me with idle chatter
And I listen smiling while my heart starts to shatter,
How I loathe the morn, how I dread the night
Why I hate life at dawn It's an ongoing plight,
My windowless castle is only that of dreams,
Only nightmares come true
Only nightmare's come true, it seems.

**Light Seekers**

I was at work once, went to the cafe for a tea,
They said 'cash only'
Obviously I had none on me
And a woman bought it for free,
I nearly cried,
That's the current state of my mind,
That's the level of fragility
That follows me
Wherever I roam,
I'm hardly happy unless I'm crying at home,
Depressing I know
But at least I don't have to fake how I feel,
Everyone thinks I'm happy and smiley all the time,
That isn't real,
That doesn't show my heart,
The majesty of my tragedy rips my heart apart,
No one knows, no one really knows,
The harder I try
The more sorrow grows,
Is there any sense in burdening another?
When I know people aren't there for each other,,
In silence I fight,
We're all in the darkness
But some of us are seeking the light.

## Mistake Or Design

There's a noise I can't explain coming from the floor below,
It seems to follow me everywhere I go,
I hear mutters in the morning and curses deep at night,
I'm haunted by shame for all the times I didn't do right,
I pass judgment on the weekends and spend my days repenting,
I feel justifiable grief for the people I was once resenting,
I have no bounds in sleep for I'm awake in another place,
Mostly in situations that further fuel my growing disgrace
There's a hammering of hands clawing, at the ceilings beneath,
Why are my desires always this much out of reach?
I try to escape but I don't get far,
I always come back to where you are,
To cope with a lack of hope I have to live in dreams,
I'd rather be the one demeaned than be the one that demeans.

**As It Is**

I miss you so hard my love
My heart cannot bear,
Being alone without you there
But in solitude I've always been,
Haven't sought to see people
Haven't myself been seen,
And I lose half a day in less than an hour
All because my life's turned sour
I cower at the pain that's sure to come,
What fun life is,
One moment in hell
The next in bliss,
My God, how can I live like this?
So when I look into these eyes,
All I see is my own demise
Beckoning me through the storm that lies ahead,
I'm shunned by the living,
I get nothing when I'm giving,
So I'm forced to walk alone amongst the dead,
I tell you I'm glad that I survived,
I'm blessed I'm even alive,
But on days when darkness persisted,
I don't wish to die, I wish never to have existed.

## The Ineffable Web

I just parted ways with my last best friend
And into the night I roam,
All I have are my thoughts and heartbeat,
The closest thing to home,
The destruction of others
My sisters and brothers
March to their pending doom,
Torture awaits in every state
It's likely worse than I assume,
I'm a spider caught in another's web
Watching my death move in,
Until roles are reversed and I watch you ebb
And it's I who failed and left you to sin,
I sit alone in this tangled snare
The corpse of my love In bits,
I'm the only person that relies on my care,
I'm shocked I survived as many hits,
Daylight brings a clean page
But the previous written remain,
And I write the same words infused with rage
Replaying and repeating the same endless pain,
At night I move to the rooftop
Where I'm lost in the eyes of space,
The only moments my torment will stop
And I cry dry tears of disgrace.

**Sins**

I had my heart ripped out at war,
I tell you now the battle wounds never healed,
The moment I fell in love I had my fate
Securely sealed and now I cry at the moon,
Alone, cold to the bone and too far from home,
Watching friends become foes in the dead of night,
Man has no will to do what's right,
He sets his sight on something and that's about it,
Wars never end, years roll by,
May not seem it but all I do is cry,
My allies only lie,
I've never known a man to love me enough to actually try,
How I wish I could fly
Away from this place,
I wish I could leave and take with me every trace,
Not even my shadow would I leave behind,
Nor a print in earth nor sand,
Just because we have eyes doesn't mean we're not blind,
Now that I fly I wish never to land,
I need to see the water, the ocean calls my name,
The ones who say they love me are driving me insane,
And no one hears me calling, screaming to silenced stars,
I only hear the sound of your name not the streets nor the sound of cars,
I present I'm fine on the outside, I'm broken deep within,
I didn't realise how conceited I was
Nor the levels in which I'd sin.

## A Distant Memory

Oh broken-hearted fool of the night,
How did your sly and mischievous soul make its way into my life?
When once all was beautiful and calm,
How alarming it is when life alters this dramatically,
Allowing decisions I refused emphatically
For such a long time,
The winding roads meandering constantly
Through heaven and hell,
I'm a soldier on a journey so that's where I dwell,
No matter what befell I always got back up,
I might take a while but I *always* get back up,
Oh the suffering and sorrow that awaits tomorrow
Is nothing of what it could be,
So I rest easy,
When life's this breezy,
It doesn't always please me
But just think how much worse it could be?
The time is near,
Soon God will be here,
And all of this will fade away,
I know I shouldn't
But I yearn for that day,
Until then I'm surrounded by lies and decay,
Pretending everything's fine
When nothing's going my way,
I sigh deeply, oh woe is me!
I pray to get through the day, the week, the month, the year,
Killing demons by extinguishing fear,

Throw it into the depths,
There's still time left,
And the rest won't even be,
Not even a distant memory.

## Please Don't Bury Me

Please don't bury me,
I know it's easier than having to see
And feeling the morbid reality,
It's been a wild ride,
But don't bury me and hide with the bad all the good,
I've done all I could
But you're hell bent on suppressing,
The thought of me,
God, I find that so depressing,
To love that hard
And let go that easily,
It makes me uneasy to know,
You're meant to love with all your heart then be fine with letting go?
I know I tainted it all, I know my mind was savage
I know every happy time's been ruined and ravaged
I don't blame you for wanting to be free,
But please don't bury *every* memory of me,
How quickly time dissolves
Every trace and every tie,
And you're with someone else
In the blink of an eye,
I don't mean to condemn,
But you can't do that unless you've buried them,
And I'm not dead
I'm alive,
This didn't have to be,
It didn't have to end this way, you didn't have to bury me.

## What Is This Life?

Oh how I miss when life wasn't this,
This accursed and wicked place!
Ever in a plight
Void of light
Searching for stars in the darkness of night,
Surrounded by rapturous claws of the ungrateful,
Overflowing with ego are the ever hateful,
With their sealed hearts
And blinded eyes,
Feigning love when really they despise,
Any good I strive for,
I'm encircled by snakes fighting all I abhor
'I can't take it anymore' I plead to my Father
Begging in fits of pain to make me a martyr,
Then repenting profusely for my ingratitude,
Praying to God to change my attitude,
From soft and weak to strong and meek,
I'm scrambling in the darkness and can't find my feet,
Oh, what is this life
When life is lived like this?

**Made To Be Loved**

Every morning I wake up and cry,
Trying to fight the thought of wanting to die,
The last thing I want is to feel such an awful thing,
To feel this worthless, feel this hopeless, to feel like nothing,
Going nowhere but into deeper depths of darkness,
Apparently I'm loved but I'm loved by the heartless,
All I have are wounds that have left their mark,
No solace in mind my thoughts are all dark,
I love love but it doesn't love me back,
So I wonder alone, lacking light in the void of black,
They say blessings are coming
And I'm sure they are,
To pluck you out, fill you with light, and make you a star,
I'll watch them sparkle next to the moon
So high above,
I wasn't made for this world,
Made for this life,
Made to be loved.

## Callous

In the early hours of a forgettable night through turrets of a city I fail to remember,
Squinting at the first glimpse of daybreak yet shivering from thrashes of November,
My eyes recoil at the sights I loathe and rejoice somehow at a watery bed,
Of the river glowing in winter light a mirage to life and now for the dead,
Music plays in tunnels beneath echoing through trees that sleep on the heath,
The dance above ground has ceased,
Never until now would I relinquish my grip of the deceased I refused to release,
No respite lies in memories nor the tales in mind replayed,
They bring not the comfort sought but a hideous reminder so cruelly displayed,
Chimes, knell's on a drunken hill hands striking time for the city,
I ask for nothing but to relinquish control from the pain that brings about my self-pity.

## Unraveling

I've been so unhappy now for far too long,
I'm not going places I'm just holding on,
Trying to make up for the things I've done wrong,
I've nothing to give,
I thought I'd follow my dreams and leave something big,
A legacy of good,
But I'm not living the way that I should,
I'm over lamenting and repenting or complaining,
I just accept my fate cause it's too damn draining,
Fighting when there's nothing to conquer,
I used to be so much stronger, I'm alone,
I wasn't made to be happy or sit atop a throne,
I lie in the shadows coddling the darkness between my trembling hands,
No man understands
The chaos and the violence,
I pray to my Father but all I get is silence,
I was once on a path now I wonder the wild,
To think life's all downhill from the time I was a child,
I've given up trying,
Everytime I try I just feel like I'm dying,
Maybe my destiny's that of death,
I can live with that,
Just obliterate me and turn me back,
To star dust, to matter, to anything but me,
I wasn't made to live,
I wasn't made to be happy.

## Unworthy

I turn to you and you turn away,
What have I done to be treated this way?
What am I doing wrong?
I've dug my own grave
I've heard my swan song,
I wasn't long for this world,
We can't all live,
We don't all have something from God to give,
How I'd love to fade away,
On a cool, sweet breeze on a warm summer's day,
To relinquish this heart,
Renounce this life and forever depart,
I know only
To get closer to you,
If I'm not doing that I've got nothing to do,
I always return
Even if I rebel,
But I remain here alone in hell,
I call on you for help from above,
I'm not worthy of life
Nor of God's love.

## Questions Of Peril

I wake up with such an intense urge to live,
To be free,
To be me in all that rigorous glory,
Filled with love and light and a burning energy,
To move within the Earth with the life God gave me,
I panic in the shackles that hold me down,
With alacrity my happiness drowns
And I remember I'm just a bird in a cage,
Whether humbled or enraged
Nothing changes my condition,
I used to trust my intuition
But I don't know anymore,
I'm sick of lamenting and wiping my eyes,
I'm sick of trying, failing and feeling this demoralised,
Feeling like by God I'm despised,
God grant me strength
And the ability to see,
To understand what's happening to me,
Why it feels I'm stagnant
Yet all I do is try,
I want to make something of myself
I don't want to die, like this.

## Am I There Yet?

I feel like an outsider looking in,
My God when will it be my turn to win?
I've been replacing every sin
With an act of good,
I don't do what I want
I do what I should
And now that's all I want to do,
All those people I loved?
They're nothing,
I only have love for you,
I once did it all out of duty
I thought my face held the peak of my beauty,
But really it all lay in my heart,
I felt you from the very start,
It was this world that buried my nature,
Lured me into sure danger,
I've been wondering alone as a stranger
But I'm tired of living adrift,
I can't bear to know there's a rift between you and I,
If I can't get close to you I may as well die,
I think of you and cry!
You're the only reason I try,
And I know I'm way too eager,
My efforts they've merely been meager,
I know I need to be patient,
But how long can I live this way?
Waiting for the day to behold you and be close,
To you my Father

To whom I love most,
I'll stand at my post
With tears streaming down my face,
I'm tired of losing the same damn race,
Yet I have faith,
Faith in the grace
That you know better,
Better than all,
I'll keep looking in
Until I'm in too,
I'll hold onto my yarn
By thinking of you.

## Mock Me Not

I hear a mocking sound high in the trees,
As I stand on my knees I raise my eyes,
The truth and the lies were set free,
Making me a still and empty entity,
I resent myself intrepidly
For all I've done to me,
This call awakens me but is this it?
Am I to walk alive amongst all I destroyed?
This living, breathing, deathly void,
I awake into dreams
I'm alive in the night
I only do wickedness yet I strive to do right,
What light is this? Coming from heaven,
What sound?
What thought?
What life?
I may not be a weapon
But I'm needed to wield the knife,
And I don't know the future
I remember not the past,
I own the present and the present moves fast,
I try to make each day,
Go my way,
Happiness doesn't stay,
And nothing here will last,
I move to death, I'm moving past
All those mocking cries.

## Not Doing So Well

I don't think I'm doing so well,
Everyone around me's thriving in hell
But I'm a victim to my vices,
Using them as coping devices
To refrain from feeling my heart,
If I did it would tare me apart,
I don't know where to start,
I walk and I run but I don't get very far,
I try and I strive, I'm an extinguished star,
My light's diminished,
It's hardly begun but for me life's finished,
I can sense my own demise,
I just have to look
To see the pain deep in my eyes,
My soul's untamed and wild.
I won't die a mother,
I'll die just as a child,
My life given to another,
I never wanted to rebel,
I'm holding on but I'm not doing so well,
No, I'm not doing so well.

## Hiraeth

I awoke from a beautiful dream, into a golden morning,
Still the past is present here,
My heartbeat quickens with a lowly warning,
I lose my eyes in what I idolise, the clouds that disfigure the sky,
But they evaporate and dissipate and like them I comply,
I've no water spare to shed a tear, nor breath to waste on wails,
I accompany life to a silent future but I'm taunted by prior tales,
I know of false angels and idols, basking in fake narcissism,
Mankind always let me down so I'm justified in my cynicism,
Dead are my confidants, not a soul on Earth do I trust,
Some days I have my moments but mostly my heart's been hushed,
I take each day as it presents itself, it's a lie if you see me smile,
I lose myself in contemplation, I'm the victim of peoples guile,
There's many events I regret of the past, does that make the playing field level?
There's no justifying the pact that's been made nor the sleeping with the devil,
Am I a worthy recipient of all that I behold?
I'm chained and shackled to the end of my days, so I pray I shan't grow old,
I awake from a beautiful dream, into a golden morning,
Still the past is present here and still this ghost is haunting.

## Blind Leading The Blind

I wake up to the consequences of destruction and shudder,
Today will be like every other
Fighting one another without any resolution,
How many times will I mount this ride expecting a conclusion
To favour my side,
When it never has,
And how can I be mad at him?
When I myself do the exact same thing?
Why do I try when I look but don't find?
I try to guide us but it's the blind leading the blind.

## Dead Weight

Why do I watch time, as if something's going to disturb those lines?
And repair these irreconcilable crimes,
I mumble curses and mask smiles
I'd walk with the rain for miles and miles,
There's nothing stiller than a strong, secure pillar,
Holding up ceaselessly the weight of its killer,
And I listen focused to your thoughts on the wrong warped and trapped behind a closed door,
The word sorry has no meaning if you keep doing the thing you're apologising for,
I'm realising more, more and more, that it didn't have to happen what happened before,
And I'm rich in the wallet but exceedingly poor,
Spare a coin to my wayward hands,
Lend a word I'm starting to feel I might understand,
I'm sick of this land, a distant fairy tale like the sea without sand,
I mumble curses and mask smiles
I'd walk with the rain for miles and miles
But I'm uselessly stiller like the ruins of a pillar
Holding up ceaselessly the corpse of my killer.

### **Filthy Fridays**

I hate filthy fridays,
It's when spiritual attack comes my way,
Every, single, friday,
Like clockwork
The burden doubles
And all the bubbles of joy I might have created,
Pops and all good dissipated,
One step forward,
Ten steps back,
I touch the light then I'm back to black,
Every filthy friday
The same spiritual attack.

## The Void Of Desolation

The many aspects of hell, them all I despise,
But the worst is seeing the pain in their eyes,
Walking the vile streets in the void of desolation,
As rejects when they're kings of a nation,
Oh the iration, a constant frustration,
An abomination to God's good creation,
When blasphemers sin with little affect,
Innately evil from a genetic defect,
So, what would you expect?
A demon's a demon no matter how fair-seeming
They seem,
I deem you a devil, so let's rise up a level,
And in the light of what's right
Let's joyfully revel.

## The Horror

It's horrific out there I tell you!
Worse than I thought,
I keep learning lessons I've already been taught
And fighting battles I've already fought,
What sort of life is this?
I'm living in hell
The darkest abyss,
I asked the questions
But your answers I missed.

## A kind Of Man

Why must people keep doing things that make me hate mankind?
Why?
Shouldn't there be something good to find?
Or are you all such selfish morons, one idiot leading the blind?
I try to find beauty in the solace of my race
But I leave them behind with heightened disgrace,
A look of defeat sprawled across my face,
A sigh of disdain and despair is all I can bear
Near the kings of my country for why would they care?
Mostly I hate how when I'm surrounded by friends and cheer,
I spend the whole time wishing I wasn't here,
And they talk and laugh to mask the fear,
And I sit,
Nodding, waving, talking bit by bit,
Hearing the streaming of legacies lost to another,
While I sit here with another stray brother,
Together but so far from each other,
All the while marking our backs
Inviting over more spiritual attacks,
Are we even human anymore?
Everyday a Godless feast,
Searching for signs of life,
All that stares back is a beast.

## When Love Is Young

My delight, what a light you are,
Back when the sun shone bright in summer,
Those were the hazy, lazy days
In youth we were just two lonely strays,
Trying to find God in two different ways,
How darkness descended slow at first,
It was too late once we were over the worst,
You caught my eye with a look that could kill,
I was just too high gone was the will,
My sweet brethren, held my hand and wiped my tears,
I cut away at my heart for years and years
And I left those pieces on the glassy, green, grass,
Mesmorised by the lights that went past,
Holding my wounds on the tip of my tongue,
I didn't appreciate love when love was young

## The Dynasty

Oh why do you gamble things you don't possess?
I guessed you'd play a feeble bet
Though you've never experienced this level of success
And you're not deterred by your growing debt,
Tragic is the sun for it doesn't shine on me,
That sums up their philosophy
And hinders your prosperity,
Clearly you don't mind entering private territory,
The same old selfish story,
Besotted and rotted by your own false glory!
I asked for help but it never came, a shame,
I'm sick of these elites, elite only in name,
Free to roam,
While I call prison my lonely home,
The only bet I've ever won the dealer had me mistaken,
And the jackpot with my winnings had somehow been taken,
Oh why do you gamble things you don't possess?
You've become something I wholeheartedly detest
And the rest is a dynasty
Made of finery
To be consumed in fire in its entirety.

## Painless

I hate to be the cause of pain,
I rather have it upon myself,
Otherwise I'm sure to go insane,
I hate to be the cause of pain,
I rather have it wash away like rain,
I rather have taken away my soul and wealth,
I hate to be the cause of pain,
I rather have it upon myself.

**LIMBO**

## Legacies

I walk down the city street just like so many before,
Burdened by what ails me and all that I endure,
I merely mean to add my verse
And set a loose another curse
Amongst them,
And just because I never sang
Or heard the rings of the songs that rang
Doesn't mean I don't possess the lyrics of them all,
Let me create and relate something
Before my inevitable fall.

## I Denounce You

I arose from the ashes to the sound of sweet music,
In a place where pain can't exist,
An eye that marvels behind the smoke,
Speaks songs you could never resist,
Of beautiful nothingness, in flames of equanimity
Where life is gone and you move through infinity,
To the waves of sound intensifying,
Leaves fall to their death beneath a mirage of gold,
Remorseless in desire through choice of defying,
Colour emanates towards the eye here behold,
On the river banks where birds skim subtly,
There's the lull of another's voice,
Professing their confession a divine narrative,
Voiding our burden of choice,
And a breeze of purity joyous in form,
Ignites the self within,
Coursing through an absent body,
Where I touch and can't feel the skin,
I arose from the ashes to the sound of sweet music,
In a place where pain can't exist,
An eye that marvels behind the smoke,
Speaks songs I'd never resist.

**Nightly Prayer**

I pray the same words into the night,
In hope they'll find your soul,
That somewhere within you'll find the light,
I pray the same words into the night,
To not give up but choose to fight,
And rise to be a whole,
I pray the same words into the night,
In hope they'll find your soul.

## Just You And I

Ah, I remember when I was young
The haven I made within the peril,
Weaving words that came from heaven,
Dreaming dreams that didn't seem far fetched,
Constantly failing but loving the tests,
Because I loved the fight
When fighting for what's right,
Now my strength it fails me daily,
Around and around like I'm going crazy,
The more I try the more I get lazy
And I miss you,
And all I endured for,
My comfort, my refuge
Just you and I,
Just you and I dancing above the sky
And nothing from life,
My life, exists,
Just my soul as a whole
Away from all this.

**Sights**

Why do wicked things pull me close
When all I want is you?
To let go of the lies and live only truth
Under this roof in which I reside,
I don't want to get mixed up with the tide
Of turmoil and disarray,
I want to listen to what God has to say,
Let the pain of the day wash away,
Be right,
Do right,
Live right,
And keep you,
Always in my sight.

## Grace

I walk empty streets and enter an empty carriage,
The train to nowhere rattles away with ease,
And I cry golden tears that go unseen,
Away from peering eyes cause of corona quarantine,
Wondering things I shouldn't wonder before work,
I can't reconcile there's two at force,
That in my blood they surely course,
Bringing sorrow and joy to every day,
But oh how these thoughts they taunt and torment,
Breathing life into things I only wanted to vent,
The wasted hours I casually spent,
Questioning things when I knew what they meant,
As if I'm hell bent on bringing about my own ruin,
You can't rely on the work from your past,
People forget that all too fast,
And so my tears are valid but far from just,
I try to let grace lead the way,
But I've failed on this and many a day,
The train to nowhere pulls in at every station,
I talk and I talk but I'm met with silence,
I've been brutally bruised by my own mental violence,
I no longer face it with trepidation,
I trust in you and your creation,
I have faith in you to build us a nation,
And I'll keep going as long as I can breathe,
Even if I wanted to I could never leave,
You stand upon patience
I fall guilty to haste,

But you check what needs checking
And bestow us with grace.

## Much Dismayed

I've been much dismayed in this general disarray,
Fighting fatigue from it all,
Oh, man was made to sicken and appall,
And that I am!
Sickened and appalled,
I'm cleaning up the mess of several studious sinners,
All prancing around like winners of morality,
A catastrophe unravels before my eyes!
I tire of these tiresome lies!
I shake my head at these shameless ways,
Seeking a path that only leads to your grave,
It's futile I tell you and I can only laugh, manically,
I've been through the motions and know them mechanically,
But I'm tired, I'm tired for it seems to never cease,
I'm diseased,
The more I move the less I move my feet,
Failing the beasts I swore to defeat
Some I've met and some I'm sure to meet.

## Disappearing Act

Blue sky you become a rainbow of colours if
I stare too long, vision gets blurred, my heart
Beats strong it feels wrong to wait atop the cliff,
Ocean above, sky in the midst, an upside down calamity
Of deceitful glory,
Since I've told myself the same mundane story
I hardly know what it could mean,
Is it possible to miss someone you haven't seen?
But I feel in your heart too intently to bear,
Until love starts to seep,
Bursting forth what I meant to share,
I stand, face covered, I weep,
Until tears cease to flow
And I pick myself up with nothing to do but go from whence I
came,
Don't call my name in the game of blame,
Judge me not,
The shame will get you one day, soon,
And when I look at the waves,
It's as if I look at the clouds on a fine summer's day,
And I see myself as I was before
I became who I am today,
My gaze taken to the sky,
As if answers lay beneath its coat,
And somewhere deep in the colour I faintly make out
The image of a cloud afloat,
Drifting to unknown territory.

## An Excuse For A Life

How beguiling your silence is,
You think I love staring into an abyss of soul-wrenching sorrow
While you idly look by,
I decry your callous soul!
Oh how I've spent my days lamenting
The same misguided tragedy,
A travesty to my wayward ways
Lost in a craze like I'm stuck in a cage,
I thought I'd been chastised out of that stage,
A tranquil humility absorbs the guile I fought so stoically for,
I adore the peace,
So when you greet me with that hardened heart,
I've worse things tearing me apart,
This behavior has no ill effect,
Except the depressing air of an ever present defect,
I'm not deterred by suffering and strife
In our excuse for a wretched life.

## Square One

I walk with ease in torrential rain but in mind my thoughts are clenched,
I hardly know if it's night or day or the cold from being this drenched,
Many a man owes their dues but I'm yet to receive what they owe,
I'd do it all for free you see but mankind isn't in the know,
How did time unravel my mind? For I'm often back at square one,
These thoughts, this work is far from fun
But I try to not let that show,
There's a heavy burden I'm willing to take yet the cost exceeds what I own,
Though I've put it off for far too long, it's now one I can't postpone,
And amidst the turmoil of a devils reign I'll promise to serve another,
To revel and revere in all I discover, I'm fine now to be this alone.

## The Concept of Liberty

Neon signs lead the way through the dreary night,
Mechanical stars that pave the way for unattainable dreams,
Inside in the eye of the storm,
In the world of shadows void of light,
Noise becomes music reverberating like the sounds of screams,
To find peace in pain drives you half insane
Yet it eases the mind,
I don't do what's good cause it's nice I do it cause it's right,
And to find solace in my own kind,
Step far away, to the gloomy edge of the precipice,
Glare down and face the eyes of doom,
Stretch the limits of immovable ability,
In sullen crowds I make my own room,
And where freedom is hindered,
I weave the threads of civil liberty,
For what it's worth on the darkened days I've always resisted,
Not in the appeasing hours of day but in a place where only night persisted,
Hinder not the extent of my words
Yet cut them out and make shapes where once none existed.

**Focus**

I'll focus on myself since my wealth of knowledge
You want not,
Enraptured with ego and pride
Hate coursing through your soul inside,
I give, I try, I strive to be patient,
I lean on the nation
But you want no part of it,
I'm just an irritation,
Even the sight of me,
I've strived incessantly,
You remain in place,
Coddling your callous heart
An angry look upon your face,
I'm living in a dead place,
I've already lost you
But we share the same space,
And I'm reminded of the pain
In plain sight of all I view,
I need to focus on myself
Instead of focusing on you.

## X

I didn't think at this timid age my heart would be filled with wrath and rage,
And when I was younger I had a plan to grow up and do all I can
But I broke,
I've watched blue forked lightning and heard life's thunder
Cause a blunder felt under sleek, sick, skin in the grips of the tundra,
I've moved mountains in my mind, the exact way that I designed
So through my eyes my vision and what I see are intertwined,
Of the purest kind,
And in this jubilance I perform my duty,
To enable me to see the beauty,
To acquiesce life's raw hand and let go of the one drenched in superfluity,
But woes, oh yes woes they remain to drill in and enforce the pain,
But wouldn't life be dull without the strain?
It seems my efforts are all in vain,
Until I take a step back and see the change,
See the range in the rainbow of light sprawled across
An evening sky,
To focus on one colour, a blasphemous lie.

**Only You**

I want to be truly alone with only you,
Far from the rest of the world and all its memories and
impressions,
I want to be purified and cleansed,
Not of myself but anew,
Alone someplace on a beach
With only you.

**HEAVEN**

## Elijah

Oh Lord, I open the curtains and yawn, the same depressing dawn,
A battlefield laden in fresh blood,
When will it be enough,
When will these children submit?
And quit the enemies who hate us so,
I don't want to say I loathe my foes, but Lord knows... I loathe my foes!
I await the storm armed to the teeth for darkness to form
While my brethren sleep,
Father, Father open the door,
I'm ready for war and if death comes a-knocking? I'll fight no more,
But I abhor these devils, on every level
Let me battle them and in death I'll revel,
For life in this world is *dire!*

Oh Elijah, Elijah
Come set them on fire!
Kill every liar
Messiah, Messiah,
You know how we tire,
We won't be complacent we'll strive to be patient
Our God loves a tryer,
We're in the gutter but couldn't get much higher,
As we look to the heavens for Elijah, Elijah,
In pursuit to salute our prince, our sire,
Come to us, come to us Messiah, Messiah.

## Searching For Love

I searched the world for love,
Alas, I found none!
That wasn't fun
Delving into the void of degradation,
There's no such thing as integration
Between light and dark,
Cause hell's left its mark
And it won't wipe off
So I call off all bets and walk with my cross,
Love yet to replace it,
The devil tried to deface it
But evil never prevails,
It wins and wins and then after that fails,
All hail the Creator!
The king!
I stand tall
Because I know him,
I searched the world for love
And found only sin,
I didn't find it anywhere
Until I looked within.

**I'll Never Let Go**

I love you old friend of mine,
We've walked every crazy road together,
I've cried, I've screamed
And everything in between
And you were there all the while,
Mile by mile I march,
I marched! To utter doom,
But you made a path
Out of the gloom
And the hell I made myself,
With you I have wealth,
Love and strength,
To walk this path at any length,
I remember our memories,
When less I knew,
Do you remember too?
Who I was the less I knew of you,
But you knew me,
And although low
It was your light I could see,
Shining invisibly in the vivid dark,
And that was that,
The rest is history,
To me you were never a mystery,
I searched for your out-stretched hand
That had been there forever,
And now that I've taken it I won't let go,
Never.

**All Paths Lead Back To You**

All paths lead back to you,
No matter how far I stray,
Whatever it takes I'm sure to do,
All paths lead back to you,
I can't deny what's true,
You answer when I pray,
All paths lead back to you,
No matter how far I stray.

**Eons and Eons**

When my thoughts fall to slumber
I awake in my mind,
Where paradise becomes the vision,
With the very last blink into I sink
Between the lines that break the division,
A beautiful light not day nor night
Blares across the wave I ride upon,
It splits into stars that move slowly yet fast
As I enter the timeless eon,
No noise to discern where the light doesn't burn
Through galaxies and dimensions unknown,
I'm light years removed from that place on Earth
Yet here is my only home,
No reason to blink nor utter a breath, No need for any ability,
A paradise broken through the alluring invoking
Of his force to create tranquility.

## Island Garden Paradise

To walk at night between summer grass unused beneath feet that can barely stand,
And the lights of the nights the mechanic stars that spill like blood from chasms of the skyline,
Tears created rivers, created seas, created oceans and your smile is the moon that clings to the waves of despair,
The rapture of laughs that sunk in lost turrets of watery dooms lying dormant beneath the white orb,
The blue eye, the skies eye, ever watching, ever present, ever taunting and protecting the mirage of grey that slips through the crevices of sunset and rises like a burnt out sound heard only in the filthy blues of a crestfallen Friday tune,
The lost sight like flames of a dragon rough and bereaved like the edges of the moon,
Still full and morose and reminding and hurting all the while,
A calmer note strikes the moment in two, split like lightning and melting in the invisible embers of time and disillusion forever unceasing and forever deceased in a memory or thought somewhere in these living dreams.

## Our Blessing

The sun used to shine so brightly
But now it's a distant glare,
I wish you were in my arms,
But for now you're no longer there,
The birdsong of morning respites me,
Then the world it tests my whims,
Yet I know where the history comes from
And we are the children of kings,
Little one show me those winter ice eyes,
I see in and through to your soul,
Now that you're in this world with us
You've made our family whole,
One never knows what life shall throw
For surely there's no point in guessing,
But you, our little darling,
Are our best and most precious blessing.

## The Conqueror And The Conquered

I've always been a soldier,
Even when young my heart was much older,
I started at the bottom but I'll never be done,
Long gone with fun, I once walked but now I run,
You can't kill righteous people,
With eyes that despise do you think we're that feeble?
A war is coming and where to go?
People should know they reap what they sow,
I started at the bottom but I'll never be done,
Bloodshed will glisten underneath a red sun,
Unprepared is the world for this much resistance,
Underestimating the extent of faithful persistence,
You no longer control the masses
You can't control existence,
All that meddling with madness
Created too much distance between
You and salvation,
I prepare for a gloomy future
To be surpassed by a redeeming bliss,
And all that once was of this cruel world,
Not one thing is there that I'll miss.

**All For You**

I fumble in the darkness
Enduring my trial,
Seeing the light all the while,
The one that guides the way,
I awake to a daunting day
But somehow my heart's at peace,
My Father respiting the beast
For his grace and love upon all,
All I do I do declare
Is for the one that drains despair,
And all the love I have inside
He loves in me what others despised,
I reach my arm up higher
Higher in the grip of yours,
And the demons are coming with outstretched claws,
Yet I laugh for I face what's true,
And all my life and all my love,
Father, it's all for you.

## Proof

How light I feel, a blessing from God,
To wake up and all that darkness gone,
After so long
Of battling that same fateful foe,
I can see again,
I can feel,
I can love,
I can do as I should,
Instead of wrath ruining everything of good,
A sound went out and my soul surely heard,
Heard the good in the fabric of the word,
Clear as the day do I see
When before it was blurred,
A horizon so far out of reach,
I kept going no matter how perturbed,
Yet how disturbed I've been!
Holding, clinging desperately
To my faith in the unseen,
I've stripped a layer of youth,
I prayed and I've heard the truth
What more proof
Is needed?

## On Those Indigo Nights

What did they say on those indigo nights all those years ago?
We used to look at the stars and make shapes from our hearts
Until dawn when the moon descended and the sun brought fresh meaning,
Erasing the past in a blink of an eye,
No man ventured to the ebb of the void but we did!
We pressed our toes nearer to the edge, slowly,
Yet our minds moved with alacrity beneath the stillness of each touch,
Too many, way too many times we fell into the fiery chasm,
Engulfed in pain and turmoil,
Blindly searching shadows for figures and finding none,
And what did we do?
We clawed our way up the crags until fingers bled and mixed with filth,
We wiped our faces and became what we hated,
We resented, then repented, then fell again,
Into doom, sleeping without shelter and seeing without light
Made a miserable wretch out of us,
So we'd cry silent, invisible tears
In the darkness, weeping as we did for our mothers
But instead seeking comfort from the sky,
The subtle iridescence of air glow
In the atmosphere soothing our juvenile whimpers,
And oh how these indigo nights saved us,
From darkness,
From solitude,
For surely the void brings only destruction.

## Sublime

Whose hand clutches at my outstretched arm?
When all others have released and relinquished their grip,
Into the light far away from harm,
In this crazy world a never ending trip,
I remember when the sun would rise,
Behind grey clouds concealing a horizon of gold
Unseen by all but my own mad eyes,
Watching the day grow from young to old,
No friends linger long enough to become allies for the cause,
Except my faithful companion who never leaves my side,
Who helps make good come to that of my flaws,
So I love what's out but also inside.

## Abhorrent Behavior

The very thing he fell in love with me for,
Is what in time he grew to abhor,
But I held on tight,
To that exact light,
That he can hate and I can adore.

**Always You**

Old friend I revere you as I fear you
As I should,
Remember the bad days?
I remember the good,
When we trail-blazed through every hideous phase of life,
Love and strife, emotions rife
We delved into the light of the moon,
Oh I swoon for you every day
When I close my eyes and pray,
Whispering words of pain and hate,
I was never happy - it's easy now to see,
Apart from when you were close to me,
And you'd hear my pleas and guide me forth
From the hell of darkness I loved before,
I didn't know what I thought I knew,
And it was never them,
It was always you.

## Devotion Island

On a very blue midnight I awoke alone
On an island somewhere in the ocean,
In the scent of summer beneath vanilla trees
I dug my feet into the sand of Devotion,
Fireflies like stars and stars like fireflies
Radiated illuminant on the beaches,
The only sounds were the waves cries
And the bleak gentle hum of everything not in ones reaches,
Where the wub-wub ceases and I can blink in time
With no fear of it wasted like back in Deny,
I'm a man of constant trouble
And trouble follows me constantly,
I've come to terms with my self-proclaimed notion
But can forget all my woes on the Island of Devotion,
Where fears and anxieties are replaced by tranquility
And peace on Island is declared as explicitly,
I breathe deep and long safe from the smoke
And relish the relief of not needing to choke
Listening to the distant sounds of summers croak,
I'm a man on a so to speak boat,
That's adrift an uncertain sea,
But problems that delve between waves and chasms
Have no chance of ever touching me,
I'm in the Lord's kingdom of respite and pause
Where I can dwell with ease on all that I've caused,
When I leave, and I always must, I return with a humble mind
I see every colour on Devotion Island but in Deny I'll always remain blind.

**Answers**

I prayed and you answered!
Do you know what that means to me?
I've been a miserable wretch for far too long you see,
And now I'm free,
Of guilt, of sorrow, fear and doubt,
I prayed for peace and you brought it about,
And I'm enraged and ashamed I didn't believe in the power
Until this hour
When before you I cower,
Not out of fear but respect in how you make sweet all that was sour,
Now I don't even know,
How I thought it hard fighting pride and ego
When all I had to do was submit and let go,
Did I doubt your ability
Through lack of humility?
Please hear my cries, I swear I apologise
For my unwavering stupidity
When you're all I have,
You're everyone and everything I love,
You're every moment worth living
And when down, you're the light above
That keeps on giving.

## Sunshine

Gloomy, gloomy clouds can't dull me today!
No way!
I've spent my life in dismay!
No man will take this joy I get to feel for this one day!
I peeled, PEELED!
Myself off the kitchen floor to get to work,
Oh how my soul it hurt!
Leaving my solitary void of sorrow
Knowing I can't wollow
But must feign a smile,
At faces who don't deserve it whose hearts are vile!
Time and time goes by,
Let it all go,
Cause I'll get mine back
In a different dimension,
Where time can be bought and lengthened,
I mustered the strength,
I'm going to bathe in the reward!
Even if soon my woe's restored,
For now I feel happy
And rare is this
To enjoy my life simply, just as it is.

## The Beach

Take me to our beach,
Where this world's far out of reach,
Here, on the beach just you and I,
To move through the palm trees and plants of paradise,
Here you suffice, all that's in my heart,
The water flows,
The waves they breathe,
I run to you and my soul's at ease,
I can be and I can be with you,
Under the sun and at home with the truth
I'm at home with you,
I can stretch my hand to yours,
Here in what's perfect gone are the flaws
And the claws of a wicked world,
Sapphire blue is that intoxicating sky,
I get lost in you until the sparkle in my eyes
Recreates the dreams I abandoned long ago,
I don't have to live in visions,
Reality grows into the substance of life,
Here, on the beach only joy is rife
Instead of woe,
And I can grab your hand and we can go,
Wherever in the Universe, to the stars that call,
It's not enough these fleeting moments,
I want it all, all the time,
To walk with you each and every day,
Not just when I'm led astray,
I want to stay here on the beach

Where the world's far out of reach,
Here, on the beach just you and I.

## Summer Daze

The dreams of youth I once possessed,
Are caught up with the beauty of summers finesse,
In the places where spaces are formed of flowers,
I'm lost in sweet thoughts for hours and hours,
Dazing and gazing at the sun and sky,
A blessing to watch birds fly by on high,
I love the ease,
The sound of the breeze,
Whistling gently through sycamore trees,
And when dusk is dark in the midst of a storm,
Have faith that clear skies form at dawn.

**Close To You**

The rain outside is pounding,
The thunder's surely resounding,
These villains have started surrounding, all that I adore,
And I'm trapped in a sickly rut,
I fight yet I don't get cut,
It may seem that I'm stuck but I cull what I abhor,
I don't feel the pain it's true,
No hurt comes my way when I feel this close to you,

As I walk the ground it crumbles,
But in the valley no man stumbles,
My heart it remains truly humbled, yet my friends don't have a clue,
I have all the friend I need,
When I feel this close to you,

In life the heart takes a beating,
It feels I'm never defeating,
My foes go on demeaning the truth I fought to secure,
And life's lost its particular appeal,
Through lack of a righteous zeal,
But from my soul you can never steal,
What I know to always be true,
That nothing else matters,
When I feel this close to you,

So take everything I needed,
From prison I've still succeeded,

He answered when I pleaded and I've nothing left to do,
There's nothing that I want,
When I'm finally this close to you.

Printed in Great Britain
by Amazon